HUNTER'S MOON

Thick smoke drifted across the
moon. An owl flapped away into the
blackness. Neil turned suddenly. He
was sure the eyes were following his
every move. Neil spun round in the
mud. Then he ran off into the night.

When Neil was gone, the watcher
returned. The fire was nearly out.
The watcher kicked the embers into
the damp grass, then stared up to
greet the Hunter's Moon.

D0494167

SHARP SHADES

HUNTER'S MOON

Look out for other exciting stories
in the *Sharp Shades* series:

A Murder of Crows by Penny Bates
Shouting at the Stars by David Belbin
Witness by Anne Cassidy
Doing the Double by Alan Durant
Tears of a Friend by Joanna Kenrick
Blitz by David Orme
Plague by David Orme

SHARP SHADES

HUNTER'S MOON

By John Townsend
Adapted by David Belbin

Malvern Campus
F
36586

Published by Evans Brothers Limited
2A Portman Mansions
Chiltern St
London W1U 6NR

© Evans Brothers Limited 2008

All rights reserved. No part of this publication
may be reproduced, stored in a retrieval system
or transmitted in any form, or by any means,
electronic, mechanical, photocopying, recording
or otherwise, without the prior permission of
Evans Brothers Limited.

British Library Cataloguing in Publication Data
Townsend, John, 1955-
    Hunter's moon. - Differentiated ed. - (Sharp
    shades)
    1. Horror tales 2. Young adult fiction
    I. Title
    823.9'14[J]

ISBN-13: 9780237535247

Series Editor: David Belbin
Editor: Julia Moffatt
Designer: Rob Walster
Picture research: Bryony Jones

This abridged edition was first published in its
original form as a *Shades* title of the same name.

Picture acknowledgements:
istockphoto.com: pp 8, 11, 15, 20, 27, 33, 36, 45,
47, 53 and 61

Contents

Chapter One

The dark never bothered Neil. Until
now. Something was there. Something
alive. It was watching him.

The beam from his torch swept
the darkness. He could see nothing,

but something was moving. Dead leaves crunched. A shiver ran down the back of Neil's neck. He took a box of matches from his pocket. He would feel safer once the bonfire was burning.

The matchbox shook in his fingers. Neil felt so stupid. He knew every inch of those woods. He'd lit bonfires after dark many times. He was used to being alone. But now he wasn't alone. He saw a pair of eyes blink.

The pile of branches was soon lit. Neil threw dead leaves into the flames. He turned to peer into the

wood. The eyes hid behind a tree. Thick smoke drifted across the moon. An owl flapped away into the blackness. Neil turned suddenly. He was sure the eyes were following his every move. Neil spun round in the mud. Then he ran off into the night.

When Neil was gone, the watcher returned. The fire was nearly out. The watcher kicked the embers into the damp grass, then stared up to greet the Hunter's Moon.

Chapter Two

Neil always wanted to work in the
countryside. His uncle paid him to
be a beater at shoots. Neil had a
sharp eye for danger. If buzzards
were near or a fox was in the woods,

Neil knew. If a stoat got through the fence, Neil was there like a shot. Jeff Barnard, the head gamekeeper, gave Neil a job. Jeff was full of old sayings. He was always right, too.

'See the water on the tip of that elder leaf? Tomorrow will be a fine day.'

It was a fine summer day when Jeff said, 'No sunbathing this afternoon if I were you, Neil.'

Neil laughed. 'Look at that bright blue sky. This hot weather's set to last, Jeff!'

Jeff shook his head. 'Robin knows best. Look at him on that log. When

he comes down here, that's a sure
sign of rain.'

The storm began at two. Neil was
amazed. He knew a lot about nature,
but still had plenty to learn from Jeff.

That afternoon, Jeff was mending
a bridge. He had a fall. Nobody

was near. Jeff had to crawl home in
the wet.

Jeff's back was bad, so Neil had
to take on his jobs. He worked all
hours, often in the dark. In the
woods. Neil was afraid. What were
those scratch marks on the oak tree?
Deep grooves, like claw marks. Why
were there splashes of blood on the
bird feeders? Then there was a smell.
It was near the broken footbridge.
The bridge where Jeff fell.

Chapter Three

The girl appeared like a ghost in the morning mist.

'Hi!' she called.

Neil was speechless.

'Lost your tongue?' she smiled.

Neil stared at her face, then at her muddy jeans and trainers. She read his mind.

'I slipped. It's very wet.'

'Are you lost?' he asked. It was a daft thing to say. She didn't seem lost.

'No. Not at all. I remember you.'

'Really?' he said.

'You were in the year below me at school. My friend fancied you.'

Neil blushed. He still had no idea who she was.

'I'm Tanya,' she said. 'Are there badgers round here?'

'Why do you ask?' He didn't trust

people who asked about badgers.
Last month, three setts were dug up.
The badgers were taken for sport.

'My project.' She waved a pencil.
There was a sketch-pad under her
arm. 'I'm an art student. I'd love to
see a baby badger.'

'It's not all you might see.' Neil
spoke without thinking. The fears
of the last few nights were getting
to him.

'What did you have in mind?'

'Oh, nothing,' he said, trying to
laugh it off.

She moved closer. 'Do you mean
the beast? Everyone's talking about it.

They say there's a panther on the loose!'

Neil had heard the rumours.
They'd been going round for years.
For the first time, he believed them.

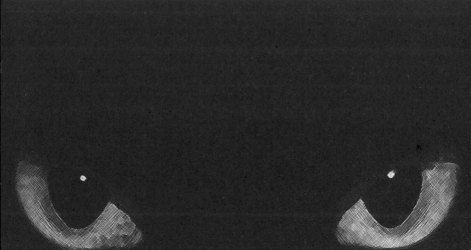

The strong smell by the bridge was from a big cat, marking out its hunting ground. Then there were the claw marks…

'You look dead serious all of a sudden,' Tanya said. 'You look better when you smile.'

She giggled. Then there was a terrible crack. A gunshot ripped right past them.

Tanya screamed.

Chapter Four

The echo hung in the air. Crows
sprang from the trees. A figure stood
on the bank. He laughed.

'I bet that woke you up!'

'You fool!' Tanya shouted back.

'My little joke.' The grinning figure walked towards them. Neil knew him. It was Joe Linsey from the kennels.

'What do you think you're doing? You could have hit someone!'

'Cool it, mate. I know what I'm doing. I was aiming for that tree, and that's just what I hit.'

Tanya turned on him.

'How did you know I was here?'

'Just keeping my eye on you, Tanya,' he said. 'The beast could be after you.' He turned to Joe. 'Keep your hands off my woman. We wouldn't like to fall out, would we?

Remember me from school?'

Neil couldn't forget. People used to leave Joe alone. He would stand in the corner of the yard and preach. He used to say he was some sort of prophet. Most people said he was mad.

'How could I forget you?' Neil said. 'Still crazy, I see.'

Tanya smiled again.

'You're dead right. I can't think what I see in him.' She giggled again.

Joe looked Neil in the eye.

'Have you seen this big cat? The sign of the beast is always with us.'

Tanya rolled her eyes.

'Here he goes. Preaching again. He'll start quoting the Bible now.'

Joe ignored her. 'Joel chapter one, verse six. "It has the teeth of a lion and the fangs of a lioness." '

Tanya reached for Joe's hand.

'He's mad but he's good with the hounds, aren't you, love?'

'They know I'm boss.' He stroked the barrel of his gun.

Neil couldn't understand what Tanya saw in Joe.

'I'm going to the hunt on Saturday. I want to paint a fox,' Tanya said, as if she'd read his mind.

Joe snorted.

'You'll need to use a lot of red when they rip it apart.'

'You could come and join us, Neil,' Tanya said. 'We meet at The Nelson Inn at 11 o'clock. It's the first hunt of the season.'

Joe sneered. 'He'll be working. He's got to keep these woods safe. It must be tricky on his own, without his boss. And lonely. When do you get time off?'

Neil didn't like his questions. Why did he want to know?

A large bird rose above the hills.

'You could sketch that buzzard,'

Joe told Tanya.

Neil said nothing. He knew Joe was testing him. It was no buzzard. It was a red kite. The local pair of red kites brought bird watchers from far and wide. But they also brought others, looking for ways to make easy money. Some would pay thousands for eggs or chicks. Only Neil knew the exact tree where the pair nested.

Some hunters were ruthless. Neil had to be on his guard.

Later that evening Neil saw how right he'd been. Earth and bracken littered the track. Another badger sett had been dug up. One of the pheasant pens was damaged. Feathers lay in the blood-stained grass.

Chapter Five

Neil had a lot on his mind. He
decided to visit Jeff.

It was already dark when Neil left
work. A pale moon peeped above
the trees. It was the moon that Jeff

first spoke about.

'On Friday you'll be able to work all night. It's Hunter's Moon. Brightest moon of the year.'

Jeff was still in pain. And he had money worries.

'I hope you're ready for the big shoot at the weekend. We've got to give them good sport this season. This is our last chance. But *Beware the nights of Hunter's Moon, When all beasts dance to another tune.* That's an old saying round here. And this year it's Hallowe'en. So take care.'

Neil had never heard Jeff speak like this before. Maybe he shouldn't worry Jeff about anything else. He had enough on his plate.

'Have you seen any sign of this big cat on the loose?' Jeff asked. 'I wish I was back on my feet to sort things out. Be on the alert, Neil. My bit of wood has rich pickings. A good poacher could strip the lot and be a few grand the richer. But that's not all...'

Before Jeff could finish, a brick smashed through the window. Glass fell like rain around them. Neil rushed to pick up the brick. It was wrapped in paper with three words on it in large letters.

BEWARE HUNTER'S MOON

There were more letters on the back.

JOE L231

They were written in blood.

Chapter Six

There was a storm that night. As soon as it was light, Neil went to look for damage. A fence was down. A fallen tree had smashed one of the tool sheds. At least the pheasant

pens were still in one piece. Just.

Behind him a twig snapped. Neil looked round. Nothing stirred. His heart raced. Was it the creature? He reached down to pick up a stick. He saw a shape on the track. His heart missed a beat. A black animal ran towards him. A voice rang out through the trees.

'Here boy!'

The labrador wagged its tail.

'Don't worry, Neil. He's harmless.' It was Mr Fenby from The Old Manor House. 'He's a bit excited. He saw something back there. Something big. I'm pretty sure it was the big cat. It made me panic, I can tell you. The hounds will sort it out.'

Mr Fenby was Master of the Hunt.

'You can't this week, Mr Fenby. Don't forget it's the big shoot.'

Mr Fenby didn't like being told what he couldn't do.

'Shame. I see there are a few trees down, Neil. A nasty storm, eh?'

Neil looked at the bag in Mr Fenby's hand.

'Oh, I hope you don't mind. I'm just getting some breakfast. Don't worry. I've kept to the public path. I haven't gone into Jeff's private wood. There are lots of chestnuts and mushrooms this year. Just the job. By the way, how is Jeff?'

'Not too good. He had a nasty shock last night. Someone hurled a brick through his window. There was a note with some sort of code. Jeff said it might be a car number plate. "JOE L231".'

'There are some strange people about, Neil. But if it said JOE, I bet he knows something about it. He's got an odd streak, that one.'

Chapter Seven

There was a lot to be done for the shoot at the weekend. The shoot had to be a success or Jeff would have to close down the woods.

Neil passed the bridge on the

bank where Jeff had his accident. Smashed wood lay on both sides of the stream. But the posts were still firm. Two had clean cuts. Someone had sawn through the supports.

Ahead of him on the path, Neil saw a sickening sight. A bright bird lay limp in a pile of leaves. The red kite was dead. It had been shot. This was Joe's work. It was time to hit back.

Neil stormed into the kennel yard. Joe was cleaning out one of the dog pens.

'I want a word with you, Linsey.' Neil waved his stick above his head.

Joe looked up sharply.

'Watch who you're shouting at, or I'll jump this wall and show you who's boss round here.'

'First you smash stuff in our wood,' Neil shouted. 'Then you saw through the bridge. You've torn up badger setts. Now you've shot the kite. You just want to scare us out, don't you? You want to get your hands on our woods.'

Joe jumped the wall.

'Prove it.'

Neil jabbed the stick at his chest.

'You think you can scare Jeff with a brick and a stupid note about

Hunter's Moon. Don't deny it. Your name was on it.'

Joe grabbed Neil's collar.

'I don't know what you're going on about. I'll give you ten seconds to get off this land.'

Neil carried on. 'Did you write it in the blood of some animal you killed? And what was it meant to mean, JOE L231?'

Joe let go of Neil's shirt.

'Interesting,' he said. 'Very interesting.'

A Land Rover pulled up at the end of the drive.

'Sorry, Neil. You'll have to wait.

That's Mr Fenby, he's come to pick me up. Some of us have to plan for the hunt.'

After a few strides he stopped and looked back at Neil.

'Try a bible. It's not JOE, you fool. It's JOEL. Chapter 2, verse 31.'

The church door was unlocked. Neil found a bible near the door. It took him a long time to find the book of Joel. He read chapter 2, verse 31.

"The sun will be turned to darkness and the moon to blood."

Tonight was Hunter's Moon. *Beware Hunter's Moon.* What did it

mean? The church clock rang twelve
times. Midday. Just twelve hours
until the Hunter's Moon would turn
to blood. The night of Hallowe'en.

Chapter Eight

Tanya was gasping for breath when she found Neil in the woods.

'I knew you'd be here,' she said. 'I've got to tell you something.'

Neil smiled. 'Come over here

while I light this fire.'

The bonfire crackled to life.

'Go on, then. What is it you need

to tell me?'

'It's Joe,' she said. 'He's really ill. I found him this afternoon. He couldn't stand up. I called the ambulance. He told me to come and tell you. Something about Hunter's Moon. He said you need to keep watch tonight. Joe said he was planning to come up here at midnight to get proof. What did he mean?'

Neil didn't want to tell Tanya how he hated Joe.

'Why didn't you go with him to hospital?' he asked.

'I can't stand Joe. It's all an act.

You could even call me a spy. I'm doing it for the hunt saboteurs at college. We're planning to disrupt the hunt on Saturday. I agreed to get inside information. I came today to get names and addresses of hunt members. I hate what Joe stands for.'

'Then you must hate me too,' Neil said. 'I rear birds for people to kill. I bet you sabs don't like that, do you?'

Tanya touched his knee.

'That's different from ripping a fox apart. Besides, you're really nice.'

'Then how about joining me here tonight? We can see what Joe was so worried about.'

Chapter Nine

'Joe's mum phoned,' Tanya told Neil.
'He's still very ill. They pumped out his
stomach and he's on a drip. They do
that to people who take an overdose.
I'm sure Joe hasn't taken drugs.'

Neil pointed at her bag.

'What's that poking out with a dirty great bin liner over it?'

'That's a secret. I took it from Joe's kitchen. Just in case.'

Neil didn't have to ask. He knew it was a shotgun. If the big cat really was out there, they might need it.

The moon was already high. They entered the woods. Tanya's hand slipped into Neil's.

'Over there!' Neil pointed at some thick bushes. 'We can hide in there.'

Soon they lay on a plastic sheet, under a sleeping bag. The gun pointed out through the twigs.

They heard it first. Then the dark figure moved through the trees. They heard something being dragged. Grunting. It was hard to see. There was a thud. The shape moved away again. Silence. Tanya squeezed Neil's hand. They waited.

The moon was high overhead. In the milky light they saw a man. He was carrying something. The footsteps came nearer. Liquid splashed around them. The smell made their eyes water. Strong ammonia. When the figure passed the bushes, Neil felt drips fall on his hand. They shone in the moonlight.

Neil felt sick. His hand was covered in blood. The sun had turned to darkness, and the moon to blood.

Chapter Ten

The figure began to dig.

'Can you see who he is?' Neil said,
but he had a good idea already.

'I'm going down there,' he said.

The man stopped digging to look

around. Neil kept to the shadows. The hole in the ground was the size of a grave. Neil stepped forward. Suddenly the man turned. He hit Neil with the spade. Neil fell. The man lifted the spade above his head like an axe. Then the shot hit him. He staggered and fell. Tanya's finger squeezed the trigger again. The figure howled. Like a beast.

Like a hunted tiger bathed by the light of Hunter's Moon.

Chapter Eleven

Today was the day of the shoot.
Jeff had told Neil to forget work.
Neil needed rest. Besides, the police
would be searching the woods. Jeff
sighed again.

'Shame Tanya won't come shooting, seeing as she's such a good shot. Pity she only gave him a couple of flesh wounds. Not enough to stop him running off. Let's hope the police have picked him up by now.'

'She saved me,' Neil said. 'Too bad we were too late to save his wife.'

Now they knew the full story. Mr Fenby from The Old Manor House had a dark secret. He was the one who threw the brick to scare them off.

'Fenby killed his wife,' said Neil.

'He couldn't bury her on his own land in case the police came looking. The next best place was the woods. He made up the panther story to stop people snooping. He used an iron claw to scratch the trees. He splashed blood about. He killed a kite and a sheep. He wrecked the bridge to get Jeff out the way. He threw ammonia so it smelt like panther pee.'

'Do you know why he waited till Hunter's Moon to bury his wife?' Jeff asked. 'It's the only night of the year when it's light enough to see in those woods without a torch. A torch can be seen from the track. He couldn't take the risk of being caught.'

'It was Joe who got wind of what was going on,' Tanya said. 'That's why Fenby got him round for a meal. To poison him.'

'Poison from under our beech trees,' Neil said. 'Those Death Cap mushrooms can be fatal.'

The phone rang and Jeff went into the hall. Neil held Tanya's hand.

'Thanks for everything,' he said. 'You not only saved my life last night, you saved our woods. Fenby wanted that land. He was waiting for us to fail. But we're not going to. I'll see to that. And all this big cat nonsense will stop now.'

Tanya smiled and kissed Neil's cheek.

'I'm going to cook a feast for us tonight. For you, Jeff and me.'

'No mushrooms, I hope!' Neil said.

Jeff came back in the room. He looked pale.

'That was my son, Bill,' he said. 'Someone found Fenby in a ditch. Dead. Bill saw him. He'd been ripped apart by someone. Or something.'

Neil looked out of the window. A

single red kite flew high above the woods. It was peaceful. But there were still secrets out there. Dark secrets known only to the night. And to the silent Hunter's Moon.

PLAGUE

David Orme

Plague

The apothecary examined my father's eyes closely. He sniffed around his mouth. My father's chest was covered with dark marks, like bruises.

'Alas, Mistress Harper, it is plague. Not all patients have the buboes. Some have dark marks on the skin. Madam, you must prepare yourself. Your husband is dying.'